P9-DGN-038

DATE			

SCARPETTA'S WINTER TABLE

—

PATRICIA CORNWELL

Wyrick & Company

Published by Wyrick & Company
1-A Pinckney Street
Charleston, SC 29401

Manufactured in the United States of America

Library of Congress Cataloging-in-Publication Data

Cornwell, Patricia Daniels.
Scarpetta's winter table / Patricia Cornwell. — 1st ed.
p. cm.
ISBN 0-941711-42-0 (cloth)
I. Title.
PS3553.0692S27 1998
813'.54 — dc21   98-35159
CIP

M

3 5 7 9 10 8 6 4 2
First Edition

To Charlie

Editor & Friend

The night after Christmas was cold and brittle, and in Dr. Kay Scarpetta's quiet Richmond neighborhood, trees were bare and groaning as they rocked in the wind. A candle burned in every window of her modern stone house, and a generous, fresh wreath of evergreen and holly was centered on the carved front door. Scarpetta had strung tiny white lights in shrubs on either side of the porch and tied big red bows on carriage lamps. She had been cooking since early afternoon, and by now her special people had gathered.

"That's enough moonshine," Scarpetta commented to Pete Marino, who was a captain at the Richmond police department and someone she had worked with for years. "No alcohol poisoning in my house."

Marino didn't listen as he poured two more jiggers of 100 proof Virginia Lightning into the blender. Each guest had his own contribution to the evening, and his was eggnog, as it was every December 26, the biggest letdown day of the year. Scarpetta always insisted that the three of them spend it together.

"You don't have to drink much of it," said Marino. "One or two snorts, and then you move on to the next thing."

"What *next thing*?" she asked, tapping a long wooden spoon on the side of the pot.

"I don't see any smoked oysters."

"In the pantry."

"Good. Wouldn't be right if you left those out."

"I never do. Doesn't matter who else likes them."

"That's the spirit," Marino said, pleased.

He was big with powerful hands capable of snatching bad people out of flight and pinning them to the ground or slamming them up against the side of a building. His red plaid shirt barely buttoned over his belly, and his thinning gray hair had a mind of its own. Scarpetta stirred the tomato sauce simmering on the stove.

"You got some wine, don't you?" he went on. "I thought I'd be civilized tonight and go with something besides beer. Here, taste this, Doc."

He poured a dollop of first-stage eggnog into a water glass and presented it to her. She sipped and her lips burned. The corn liquor warmed her throat all the way down on its way to heating up her stomach. Thoughts loosened. Much that had been vague and formless sharpened into focus.

"Wow," said the intrepid chief medical examiner of Virginia. "That's it. There will be no argument. Nobody's driving anywhere tonight. In fact, no one's going out of the house."

"I haven't finished mixing up everything, so it will be a lot better when I'm done. Plus it's got to sit for a while. You're safe for a couple hours, long enough to get your pizza going, because don't worry, Doc, ain't no way I'm letting you out of making that since you only bother maybe once a year."

It was true that Scarpetta rarely had time to spend half a day in the kitchen, and although pizza was not a conventional holiday dinner, in her case it was an unforgettable one. Her specialty pie was a unique blend of Italy, Miami, and her own originality. No one who had ever sat at her table had gone away unchanged. Scarpetta cooked with warmth and imagination. The good doctor's concoctions were meant to soothe and heal and make you feel less alone. When she gave you a meal, she gave you herself.

"Where's the eggnog?" Lucy Farinelli called out from the great room.

She was a special agent with ATF and Scarpetta's only niece.

"Hold your horses!" Marino called back.

"I want it now."

"Tough shit!"

"What then?"

"A couple hours!"

"No way my horses can wait that long!"

"No eggnog before its time!" Marino thundered.

"Then I'm going running. All this frustration! OHHHH!"

"Aunt Kay says you can't leave the house!"

Lucy secured her Sig Saur 9mm pistol inside a butt pack, buckling the strap snugly around her waist. She walked into the kitchen and hugged her aunt from behind. Scarpetta smiled as she continued stirring. Lucy made a face at Marino.

"Remember the first time Marino made his eggnog for us?" Lucy reminded them. "Wild Turkey, and lots of it. Red food coloring—for Christmas, of course. Whipped cream and peppermint candy sprinkles on top, served in frosted beer mugs. With those rather disgusting chocolate cupcakes you made." She pointed at Marino. "Green icing, little Christmas trees made out of cocktail toothpicks stuck in the middle of each one—and they were raw in the middle!"

"You're making me ill," Scarpetta exclaimed.

Lucy's laughter was loud and out of control. She held her stomach, hopping around the kitchen on one foot or the other as she howled and her aunt stirred.

"And he glued little red hots on the trees. Like ornaments. Put little stars on top. Like you get in the first grade for perfect attendance!" Lucy could barely talk, her eyes streaming as she laughed and shrieked.

Marino scowled at her.

"Everybody's got to start somewhere," he said.

MARINO'S CAUSE-OF-DEATH EGGNOG

This night he was expecting to serve three people, but it was his nature to make more of everything than was either healthy or necessary. One could look at him and deduce his *modus operandi* with no further evidence than his flushed face and considerable size. He began with a dozen eggs, cracking each with violence. Yokes went into the blender and whites went into a stainless steel mixing bowl. He blended the yokes and folded in a pound of powdered sugar.

Although most of the *hoi polloi* prefer dark rum or bourbon in their eggnog, Marino gives business to the Virginia economy and is a patron of a small family-owned distillery that makes moonshine. If you're shopping for first-rate corn liquor, you need to consider a few points. It must be legal, the still regularly inspected by ATF. It is important that copper pipes and kettles and filtered water are part of the process and that high-grade corn is used. The good stuff is rather much like combustible, mind-altering vapors. Marino likes his corn liquor in a shot glass now and then, but it is also quite compatible with eggnog and gives it a slightly different character. Marino's eggnog is for outlaws and those who war against them. It will fire you up or shut you down. If you're not used to it, it is not recommended unless you don't plan to move far or quickly from one spot for at least twelve hours.

At this stage, Marino's mixture needs to be held in custody inside the refrigerator until eggy flavors settle down and finally give in to the strong arm of alcohol. At five o'clock, while Lucy was taking her time stretching and dressing for the cold in front of the fire and Scarpetta was adding more fresh oregano to her sauce, Marino removed the blender from the refrigerator. He poured his starter eggnog into the large stainless steel bowl and with a hand mixer beat in two quarts of whipping cream. While Scarpetta wasn't looking, he splashed in four more jiggers of Virginia Lightning. He returned his spirited refreshment to the refrigerator, where it would serve hard time a little longer.

An hour later, Lucy was still running along West End streets and Scarpetta was taking a break, drinking hot cinnamon tea at the kitchen table. Marino whipped egg whites until they were stiff but not dry and blended peaks of them into the bowl. He added the egg mixture, constantly churning with the hand mixer until his brew was frothy. He poured a glass for Scarpetta and himself, liberally sprinkling both with cocoa powder.

"Merry Christmas," he said, touching her glass. "Maybe next year will be better."

"What was wrong with this one?" she wanted to know.

"I can't believe Lucy's out there running in the dark. You know it's dangerous, Doc. It's not like you got streetlights around here, and the sidewalks are all cracked up and pushed up with roots. Not to mention the way most of your neighbors drive. The little hot shot thinks nothing can hurt her."

"And who's talking?"

"Yeah, I'm here, aren't I? A hell of a lot longer than she's been."

"I believe Lucy can take care of herself," Scarpetta said.

*L*ucy's breathing was frosty blasts in perfect rhythm as she ran along Sulgrave Road in Windsor Farms, the sound of her Nikes light on pavement as she perspired in the night. Colonial lanterns and lit-up windows did not push back the darkness or show her the way, but she had run this route since high school during the many holidays and vacations spent with her aunt. After four miles Lucy was in a meditative state, her mind free to attach itself to whatever it would. This wasn't necessarily a good thing.

Although she seemed cheerful enough, she was not in the best of spirits. Typically, she had spent the holidays avoiding her mother, who had not raised her, really, and had never made Christmas anything but an empty stocking wilted on the hearth. Lucy ran harder, sweat trickling beneath her turtleneck as anger heated her up and propelled her deeper into the black shadows of antebellum trees.

Her mother had sent her another scarf for Christmas, this one navy blue with fringe and once again, her initials monogrammed in a corner.

The monograms made it difficult for Lucy to donate the scarves to thrift shops or the Salvation Army, and, of course, this was her mother's point. Her mother's gifts were always self-centered and controlling. She did not care what Lucy wanted or who she was, and Lucy did not need another scarf for the rest of her life. She did not need another pocketbook or manicure kit or delicate watch with a stretch band. She was a federal agent who shot pistols and MP5's and flew helicopters. She ran obstacle courses, lifted weights, worked arson cases, made arrests, and testified in court.

Her mother, Dorothy, was so different from her sister Kay that Lucy did not see how they could have come from the same parents. Certainly Dorothy's IQ was more than adequate, but she had neither good sense nor judgment. She did not love herself and could not care for anybody else, no matter how hard she tried to fool people. Lucy would never forget her graduation from the Federal Law Enforcement Academy in Glynco, Georgia. Aunt Kay and Marino had been there. Lucy's mother had driven halfway there before turning around. She had sped back to Miami as she and her latest lover fought on the car phone.

Lucy kicked up her pace to seven-minute miles, her long strides closing in on her aunt's home. It bothered Lucy that Scarpetta was flying to Miami the following morning to visit her mother and Dorothy. Scarpetta would not return until the weekend, and Lucy would be alone through New Year's. Maybe she could get caught up on some of her cases.

"You sure you don't want to go with me? It's never too late," Scarpetta said, when Lucy walked into the kitchen, breathing hard, cheeks rosy.

"Oh, it's too late, all right," Lucy said, yanking off wool mittens.

"Taste this. Maybe a little more basil?"

Scarpetta dipped the wooden spoon in her special sauce and offered a taste to her niece. Lucy blew on the steaming sauce, touching it to her lips, taking her time as flavors played music on her tongue. She opened a bottle of Evian.

"I wouldn't do another thing to it," Lucy said with a heavy heart.

Her melancholy had intensified the instant she had walked into the house and noticed her Aunt Kay's luggage by the front door. Apparently, Scarpetta had finished packing while Lucy was running.

"It's not too late," said Scarpetta, who knew exactly how her niece was feeling. "You've got another week off. I worry about you being by yourself. This house can be awfully empty sometimes. I should know."

"I'm by myself all the time," Lucy told her.

She opened the refrigerator. She spied Marino's wicked eggnog and looked forward to being overcome by it.

"Being alone during the holidays is different," Scarpetta went on. "And yes, you've done that before, all too often. And never with my blessing."

She stripped more fresh basil from stems, sprinkling the herb into her sauce, stirring as she talked.

"If you refuse to deal with your mother and grandmother, there's not a thing I can do about it," she said. "But you can't hide forever, Lucy. There's always a day of reckoning. Why put it off? Why not see them for what they are and move on?"

"Like you've done?" Lucy said, as anger crept forth from hidden places in her heart.

Scarpetta set down the spoon. She turned around and looked her niece in the eye.

"I should hope you would figure it out long before I did," Scarpetta quietly said. "When I was your age, Lucy, I didn't have anyone to talk to. At least you have me."

Lucy was silent for a moment. She felt bad. So many times in her life she had wished she could take back a rude remark, an unfair accusation, a bruising insult, all directed at the only person who had ever loved her.

"I'm sorry, Aunt Kay," she said.

Scarpetta knew she was and had been before.

"But, well... Why should I go down there and be victimized?" Lucy started in again. "So I can thank her for another goddamn scarf? So she can ask me about my life? She doesn't even know I have a life, and maybe I don't want her to know. And maybe I'm not going down there so I can let her make me feel bad one more time in my life."

Scarpetta resumed cooking.

"You shouldn't let anyone make you feel bad, Lucy," she said. "I agree with you. But don't go off into stubborn isolation, spending morning, noon, and night on your computer or at the range. Share yourself with someone. That's what this time of year is all about. You're in the driver's seat now, not your mother or anyone else. Laugh, tell tales, go to the movies, stay up late. Friends. You must have one out there somewhere."

Lucy smiled. She had more than one, really.

"Invite them over here," Scarpetta offered. "I don't care who. There's plenty of room and plenty to eat."

"Speaking of that," Lucy said, "when are we eating and what's for dessert?"

Heavy footsteps were followed by Marino's rumpled self. He looked sleepy, his shirttail out, shoes off.

"It's 'bout time you got back, Miss ATF," he grumbled to Lucy. "You been holding up the eggnog."

He served it in whiskey tumblers, and they drank a toast to another year together.

SCARPETTA'S HOLIDAY PIZZA

Don't even consider creating this overwhelmingly hearty and delicious pie unless you have plenty of time and are willing to work hard in the spirit of unselfishness. This is a meal that is meant to make others happy. You don't go to all this trouble for yourself, and chances are, when your art is complete, you will probably be too weary to enjoy it unless there are leftovers for the following day, and usually there aren't.

Begin with shopping. Some of what you need requires visits to specialty shops or grocery stores that offer a variety of gourmet produce and imported cheeses. One of the most important ingredients that separates Scarpetta's pizza from all others is the whole milk mozzarella she uses. This comes in balls packaged in brine, and approximately four balls ought to be enough, but that's up to you, depending on how thick you like your cheese and how many pizzas you plan on making. Do not use skim mozzarella! You will also want to pick up half a pound or so of fontina and Parmesan. Flour is very important. Scarpetta has been known to stop at bagel stores and talk proprietors into selling her five or ten pounds of very high gluten flour. She likes her crusts crisp on the outside and chewy on the inside. You will need yeast.

As for the filling, you are in charge and can use whatever suits your taste. Scarpetta has her own choices, and for her post-Christmas blast she has a tradition, her own way of saving the best for last. It is a symbol of something better to look forward to, no matter the attitudes of neighbors wheeling out mountains of Christmas trash, making resolutions about exercise and diets, and saying good-bye to relatives they scarcely ever see.

Scarpetta includes the following on her shopping list: green peppers, onions, fresh herbs such as oregano and basil, fresh mushrooms, artichoke hearts, lean ground beef, pepperoni, smoked oysters, Italian sausage, crushed tomatoes (Progresso if you don't have fresh or canned homegrown), olive oil, fresh garlic, and the cheeses already listed. It is very important to remember that both the mozzarella and the vegetables will produce a lot of water when cooked. Therefore, we must take care of this problem in advance. Begin the night before by wrapping the balls of mozzarella in cheesecloth (or towels) and storing them in the refrigerator. Some of the liquid will be absorbed.

Chop and lightly cook the vegetables. Drain them in a colander, pressing out all liquid. (The broth can be saved for soup or stew.) Put vegetables in a large bowl and allow to cool. Mix in grated Parmesan and fontina cheeses. Now it's time to start the sauce. It's really very simple. Mix crushed tomatoes with herbs and plenty of pressed garlic and a few drips of olive oil. Allow to simmer. Begin working on dessert.

Without fresh limes, don't bother. Scarpetta is a hanging judge on this matter. The key lime tree in the backyard of her childhood home in Miami once bore an

abundance of her favorite citrus fruit, and when days were hard and unyielding, Scarpetta would absent herself from the house to be soothed in the sunlight of the yard, where the solitary tree, not much taller than her father, leaned against the chainlink fence.

She would fill her pockets with key limes and gather them in her skirt. Scarpetta made key limeade and pies, and everybody felt just a little bit better. She carried key limes to her neighbors when she was hurting, lonely, and sad.

Her family had just the one tree, and Scarpetta thought of it as hers. It began to die when she was in her late teens, and she consulted a number of greenhouses, horticulturists, the Department of Agriculture, and even a plant pathologist at Cornell, where she spent her undergraduate years. There was a citrus canker, she was told. It was wiping out thousands of key lime trees in south Florida.

She doused her tree with micronutrient spray and cleaned out the dead wood. She made certain the roots weren't being damaged by the lawn mower or the trunk wasn't being rotted by standing water. Her tree continued its decline, lesions in the stems, leaves turning yellow and drifting to the grass. Scarpetta's tree died long before she gave up on it. She would not let her mother cut it down.

These days, not surprisingly, key limes are very difficult to find, thus making the dessert all the more rare and wonderful. Scarpetta gets her limes from Florida Keys Key Lime Products by making generous donations to the Marine Resource Development Foundation, in hopes that science might yet save the precious fruit. She usually orders half a bushel a month and freezes the juice, which is why she happened to have some on hand the day after Christmas when she entertained Marino and Lucy. Scarpetta thawed half a cup, which also included a hint of grated rind.

Her crust is a very basic mixture of two cups of all-purpose flour kneaded with two-thirds a cup of softened butter. Sprinkle a little water and spread the dough paper-thin in a pie pan. Bake until a light golden brown.

Mix the key lime juice with one can of Eagle Brand condensed milk (it works as well as anything made from scratch). Add a touch of salt and two barely beaten egg yolks. Stir until thickened. Pour the filling into the pie shell and lick the spoon and swipe the sides of the bowl with your finger when no one is looking. Don't waste a molecule of it. Whip up a quick meringue using the two leftover egg whites and two tablespoons of sugar. Beat until stiff but not dry and spread in thick peaks over the pie. Bake for maybe fifteen minutes until lightly brown. Return your attention to the main course.

By now your sauce should be getting very thick and rich. Continue to simmer and stir, and at least forty-five minutes before you're ready to assemble what everyone is impatiently awaiting, place a pizza stone in a very hot oven. Begin the crust by mixing one teaspoon of salt, a shake of sugar, and one teaspoon of active dried yeast with maybe a fourth of a cup of warm (but not hot) water. When frothy, add several cups of the high-gluten flour and a tablespoon of olive oil. Mix and knead on a floured surface for a good ten minutes. Place in a greased bowl and cover with a towel. Let this rise in a warm place.

Scarpetta favors a very simple salad of arugula or Boston lettuce, or whatever mixture of greens you wish. She might add tomatoes and shaved carrots and diced celery, but nothing more. Her dressing is a hearty red wine vinegar mixed with olive oil, pressed garlic, fresh ground pepper, and oregano. For the more robust appetites, she might add crumbled feta cheese. Do not toss the salad with the dressing until you are ready to call your guests to the table.

Now we are ready to create our pizza. When the dough has doubled in size, knead it some more, using your knuckles to press it out to the edges. Swipe olive oil on the pizza stone and center the dough on it, being careful not to make contact with the stone or set it on the wrong surface, as it is extremely hot. Spread a generous layer of sauce over the crust, followed by at least an inch of the meat/vegetable/cheese mixture. Squeeze the balls of mozzarella, removing as much fluid as possible. Pinch off pieces and place them over the top of the pie. Cover cookie sheets with aluminum foil and place on the second rack of the oven, as the pizza will drip no matter what. Place the stone on the top shelf, baking your pizza at the highest setting. Cook until the cheese is browning. Remove from the oven and allow to rest a moment as you serve the salad and pour a nice red burgundy. If white or red makes no difference, a Puligny-Montrachet is crisp and cleansing. You will have to eat Scarpetta's holiday pizza with a knife and fork.

On this night after Christmas, it was quiet all through the house as Scarpetta's guests sat around her table and began to eat and drink. After several lusty moments, Marino spoke first.

"Anybody don't want their oysters, you can hand 'em over here," he said.

"And how are we supposed to extract them from everything else?" Lucy wanted to know.

"Pick 'em out. Assuming your fingers are clean."

"That's gross."

"Who's in charge of music?" Scarpetta asked.

The three of them looked at each other as they ate, then Marino scooted back his chair. He got up and went to the CD player, red-checked napkin tucked into the front of his shirt. He put on Patsy Cline.

The New Year began with a chasing out of the old and a reckoning of what was to come. For Lucy, this meant brunch on January 2. It was raw and barely snowing in Richmond. She had followed her Aunt Kay's advice and had invited friends to drop by. Scarpetta was still visiting her mother in Miami, and therefore was not present either to supervise or indulge in her niece's culinary talents.

"Who wants eggs?" Lucy asked her visitors, all from various federal law enforcement agencies.

"What kind?"

"Chicken eggs," said Lucy.

"Very funny."

"Scrambled," Lucy told the truth.

"Okay."

"I thought you were making Bloody Marys," said an FBI agent whose fourth transfer had brought her to the Washington Field Office in our nation's capital, where it was not possible to catch up with crime.

"What about bacon?" Lucy asked.

She was in her aunt's kitchen, with all of its stainless steel appliances and overhead copper racks of Calphalon pots and pans. Lucy was busy snatching eggs, bacon, milk, English muffins, and jars of V-8 juice out of the refrigerator. A fire was lit in the great room, and snow was scattered, small, crazed, and cold beneath a thick gray sky. It wasn't likely Lucy and her friends were going anywhere this day. Lucy was a bold and physical *get-out-of-my-way* kind of cook. Her recipes had never been written down and tended to change as she did.

LUCY'S BLOODY MARYS

Start by getting out a large glass pitcher. Fill with as much V-8 juice as the crowd demands. Juice whole lemons and limes (this morning she used two of each and included the pulp), and add several tablespoons of the freshest horseradish you can find. Dash Worcestershire, hot pepper sauce, and fresh ground pepper to taste. Get out the salt if you want. But don't forget vodka. In a perfect world, Skyy, Ketel One, or Belvedere are Lucy's preferences. But Stolichnaya or Absolut are good, and frankly, with all this seasoning, you can use just about anything. Keep vodka and glasses in the freezer.

Stir well and chill in the refrigerator. Lucy garnishes her drinks with a stalk of tender celery and two large green olives and a wedge of lemon skewered on a toothpick. She never uses ice because it dilutes, resulting in a weak, rather disgusting looking Bloody Mary. It is better not to drink too many of these before you fire up the grill and begin cooking.

LUCY'S FRIENDLY GRILL

Mix eggs, milk, salt, and pepper, to taste. Whip until frothy. Heat up the grill. Scarpetta avoids propane gas, preferring charcoal for reasons of safety and flavor. Pour egg mixture into a simple cake pan lightly coated with oil or whatever serves the same purpose. Place the pan, strips of thick bacon, and English muffins on an upper rack of the grill. Cover with the lid to smoke. You will have to rearrange and turn the bacon fairly often, as the grease will drip and flame (adding to the flavor if you don't let matters get out of hand). Cook until obviously done. Remove and pat bacon free of grease. Serve immediately.

After eating, clean up right away because later you won't feel like it. Keep the fire going, and perhaps the snow will begin to stick and neighborhood

children will come out to play. You can watch them through the window and remember when you were that age and praying there would be no school the next day. Hopefully, you have friends over, too. Tell them they can't go anywhere because of the weather. Talk all day. Share stories and dreams, and keep the cold away.

Lucy's friends decided they were snowed in and it would be wise to stay over. It was a perfect night indeed for one of Scarpetta's soups. She keeps a good supply in her freezer, because it is her efficient tendency to cook great vats of soup at once. Lucy scanned freezer shelves of containers precisely labeled and properly sealed.

"You guys hungry?" she called out to her buddies.

Stretched out in the great room, made sleepy by the fire, they were in the midst of recounting embarrassing moments they had endured during their new agent days at their respective law enforcement academies.

"Starved!"

"Shit, you can't be. You've been eating all day."

"I have not."

"Then where did all the Triscuits go? And the Vermont cheddar? And the peanuts?"

"Anyway, like I was saying, here I was firing away on the range, cartridge cases flying everywhere, and one of them goes down the front of my shirt. And you know how hot they are."

"Ouch!"

"I started jumping around, trying to shake it out."

"Not a good thing when you've got a loaded gun in your hand."

"How 'bout something light with chicken?" Lucy called out.

That was fine with everyone.

SCARPETTA'S WHOLESOME CHICKEN SOUP

Drip several teaspoons of extra, extra virgin olive oil into a pot that is big enough to accommodate the volume of soup you wish to make. Scarpetta tends to use pots that hold at least sixteen quarts. Place skinless, boneless chicken breasts on a cutting board. Do not use wooden cutting boards  because they are more difficult to clean and can harbor salmonella and its mutants. She prefers ceramic or hard plastic. Dice chicken with a very sharp knife, keeping fingers well out of the way of the blade.

Turn burner on medium. Drop chicken into the pot to brown. Next, dice the mildest onions you can find. She always uses Vidalia onions when they are available, but she does not overwhelm this delicate soup with them. Other vegetables that usually go into this healthy dish include celery, carrots, fresh sliced mushrooms, red bell peppers, and chopped fresh spinach. Next, pour in at least four cans of fat free chicken broth.

Season with a generous number of bay leaves, and salt and pepper to taste. Allow to simmer for several hours, tasting now and then to fine-tune the seasoning. Scarpetta often adds a splash or two of sherry, and typically serves the soup in deep earthenware bowls. Homemade sourdough or multigrain bread is a nice companion to this meal. If you wish to make the soup heartier, you can add rice or risotto, or her favorite, conchiglie.

She recommends a light-bodied white wine, unless, of course, her motivation for serving you soup is that your digestive system is irritable or you are recovering from a cold or the flu. Then alcohol is taboo because it compromises the immune system, lowering one's defenses rather much as it does in all other situations in life. Assuming wine is not unwise, her choices are Chablis or Pinot Grigio. If you are in the mood for a slightly fuller bodied wine, a dry Chardonnay such as Cakebread or Sonoma-Cutrer is a fine idea.

Meanwhile, Scarpetta had meals of her own to prepare at her mother's Miami home. The weather there was considerably different from Richmond's on this second day of the New Year. The sun was warm enough to sit outside, and after falling asleep several times in a lawn chair near the dead key lime tree in the backyard, Scarpetta was infected by the guilt she always felt when dealing with her mother. The grass was so thick it almost did not give beneath Scarpetta's weight when she walked across it, heading inside.

"Mother?" she called out.

There was no answer, and Sinbad, who was both sinful and bad, tangled himself in Scarpetta's feet. The cat was a cross-eyed hybrid Siamese and knew Scarpetta did not like him and never had. Thus, Sinbad was overly attentive.

"Please move."

Scarpetta nudged the cat out of the way. He was purring loudly.

"Mother?" she called out again. "Sinbad, now I mean it, goddamn it!"

The kitchen counter was spotless, the sink empty of dishes, because of Scarpetta's guilt. She opened the refrigerator as the toilet flushed down the hall.

"Mother? What do you want for dinner tonight? Sinbad, I'm warning you!"

"Don't yell at the cat!" yelled Mrs. Scarpetta, who was very old and languishing in bad health, as she had been for years.

"I'm going to the store, I guess," Scarpetta said to the empty hallway as water ran in the bathroom sink and a cabinet door slammed shut.

"Get toilet paper," Mrs. Scarpetta yelled again.

"What about Dorothy?"

"What about her?"

"Is she going to eat with us?" Scarpetta hoped the answer was *no*.

The loud talk went on as her mother carried the conversation into her bedroom and Sinbad butted Scarpetta's leg.

"I think she has a date," Mrs. Scarpetta replied, adding one more detail. "I told her to bring him by."

Sinbad bit Scarpetta's left ankle. She did not kick him hard, but made her point. Scarpetta drove her mother's Toyota to the local Winn-Dixie, and at times like these she knew how easily she could pick up smoking again. In fact, she experienced unbearable lust as she passed racks of Marlboros, Salems, Dunhills. She would cook a bad mood meal.

SCARPETTA'S BAD MOOD SHOPPING

This always involves pasta, because a requirement on such occasions is to prepare a dish that consumes Scarpetta's energy, emotions, and attention. She moved with purpose through the dairy section and bought a carton of large eggs, opening the top to make certain none were broken. One was, and she excavated until she had better luck, carefully setting the eggs inside her cart. She searched for a wedge of Parmesan cheese.

She added a two-pound bag of all-purpose flour to her groceries, and next spent studious minutes in the produce section. Around her, people were speaking Spanish and Portuguese. Many were buying plantains, pineapples, papayas, limes, leeks, green chiles, and pimentos. Scarpetta was interested in garlic, broccoli, shallots, asparagus, carrots, 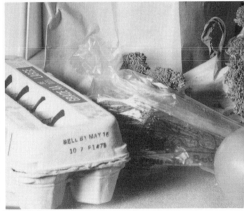 basil, and zucchini. She could have added heavy cream to this dish, and meat, such as chicken or prosciutto, but a rich, high calorie supper would only have further darkened the gathering storm clouds inside her. Although she was not inclined to please her mother at this moment, she remembered the toilet paper. Last, she bought a six-pack of Buckler non-alcoholic beer, knowing full well that Scotch, Irish whiskey, or wine would make her depressed or curt.

Most of the drive home was spent on West Flagler Street behind a red Plymouth Horizon with a license plate dangling by a twisted coat hanger. A side window was broken out and covered with a square of cardboard; the car was obviously stolen, as were so many in Miami. Scarpetta would have gotten far away from it had traffic permitted. A Mercedes with purple-tinted glass almost rear-ended her at the next traffic light, and a Porsche gunned past a Jeep, both drivers making obscene gestures at each other and screaming in foreign languages. The sun was directly in Scarpetta's eyes.

Her mother's neighborhood was in the southwest part of the city, not far from Our Lady of Lourdes Academy, where Scarpetta had gone to school and impressed the nuns. She reached the house without incident and climbed out of the car. Since her heartfelt concern for the environment had prohibited her from selecting plastic bags when asked by the cashier, the paper bags rattled as she carried her purchases through the front door. Immediately, she noted that the burglar alarm was not set.

"Mother!" she called out yet one more time this day. "You know to leave the alarm on STAY."

"You worry too much," came the reply from the bedroom. "I was taking a nap. I wish you wouldn't nag."

"Home invasions, burglaries, rapes. They don't just happen after dark."

Scarpetta made her way past the old Baldwin upright piano which her mother hadn't played since the last time it had been tuned, whenever that might have been. A lamp was on, but didn't do much good because her mother usually kept the draperies closed, and a clock ticktocked loudly from the wall. The pale blue carpet was worn and darkened with stains from the decades, and porcelain figurines of courting couples and elegant ladies from lost eras were strategically placed. Nothing had changed much, really, since Scarpetta had been a child.

Those years had been painful and scary, and the shadow of them always settled over her whenever she came home. Her father had lingered five years with leukemia before dying in the master bedroom down the hall, where her mother, this minute, was shoving coat hangers around in the closet. Scarpetta had learned to take flight into overachievement, for even making friends was hard when one was intelligent and sensitive and stunned by loss. Early on, she had cooked, cleaned, and managed the family budget while her sister wrote self-absorbed poems and stories and became increasingly addicted to boys.

Scarpetta set the bags on the counter by the sink and began removing her purchases. She washed vegetables and peeled and chopped, and an hour later Bach was playing on the classical station she always tuned in to whenever she was home, and a ball of three-egg pasta dough was peacefully resting beneath a bowl. A pot of water was ready on the stove, and a skillet glistening with olive oil awaited vegetables. She had begun to grate Parmesan cheese when her mother appeared and sat at the kitchen table before the window overlooking the backyard. Scarpetta had opened the curtains. It was getting dark out.

"What have you been doing?" Scarpetta asked, as she briskly worked the hard cheese over the grater.

"On the phone."

Mrs. Scarpetta rattled the newspaper, scanning the obituaries and feeling apprehensive when she noted that someone else her age had died.

"Gloria is ready to shoot Jose," Mrs. Scarpetta commented.

"Again?"

"I don't know why she puts up with him."

"Oldest story in the world," said Scarpetta, as she checked on the dough. "It's called dysfunction."

"You should know."

Mrs. Scarpetta turned to the editorial page, shaking the section as if it had misbehaved.

"I never understand these cartoons. Do you, Katie? The political ones. Who is this, anyway? Some communist, I guess, riding a missile like a cowboy."

Scarpetta was hurt by the reference to the romantic choices she had made in life, but she kept her feelings to herself. It was true she had not picked well when she had married Tony. She had been out to wound herself when she had fallen in love with Mark, and then fallen in love with him again many years later after she was divorced and he was a widower. Benton Wesley had broken her heart, and she had learned that nothing is ever right when a relationship begins as an affair. Although his wife eventually left him for reasons that had nothing to do with Scarpetta or him, the knowledge of what she and Benton had done had been a stain, a cracked window pane, something forever broken in the life they eventually built together. Now, he was gone, too.

SCARPETTA'S BAD MOOD PASTA PRIMAVERA

She set a colander in the sink and dusted a cutting board with flour. She readied the pasta machine she had given her mother several Christmases ago. It was a simple Rollecta 64 made in Torino, Italy, and the best *macchina per fare la pasta* Scarpetta had ever used. She set the noodle width and turned a knob to narrow the opening between the smooth rollers, and soon she was working with sheets of pasta so light and thin they were translucent. She rolled them up and cut them by hand into tagliolini. This she did expertly and swiftly because she was very skilled with knives. Rarely did Scarpetta cut herself. She had good reason to be very careful in this day of mutant viruses and vicious infections.

"What time is Dorothy coming over?" Scarpetta forced herself to ask.

"She was supposed to be here fifteen minutes ago," her mother answered, rattling the paper loudly.

Her breathing was labored from a life of smoking that had eventually hospitalized her with emphysema.

"Mother, would you like me to get your oxygen?" Scarpetta asked.

"No."

Sinbad languidly strolled into the kitchen. He stopped and gave the chef a crooked stare. His tail twitched. Scarpetta began heating the skillet. She opened the refrigerator and found a Buckler she poured into a glass.

"Well, dinner will be ready in ten minutes," she said. "Take it or leave it. If we waited for Dorothy every time she was supposed to show up, we'd turn into skeletons."

Her mother sighed. Sinbad squeezed himself between Scarpetta's feet as she turned on the burner to heat the water.

"How about boiled cat over pasta," Scarpetta said, booting Sinbad out of the way yet one more time in life.

"YUCK!" Mrs. Scarpetta protested with disgust. "How can you say such a thing?"

Scarpetta began crushing cloves of garlic and sautéing them with the vegetables.

She stripped fresh basil from its stems and sprinkled it in, adding salt and ground pepper.

"This is going to be light and healthy," Scarpetta said, knowing full well how her mother would react to this.

Momentarily, Scarpetta felt no guilt about not pleasing her mother, who did not believe in healthy food and was offended by it and took it personally. Scarpetta had learned long ago to take care of herself, to alleviate pain, and not be victimized. With her family, she would take but so much. She had been down here for almost a week. Frankly, she'd had enough, her disk was full, her nerves overloaded, she could take no more.

"What about meatballs?" her mother complained. "I can't believe you aren't serving sausage, prosciutto, or something."

"Not tonight," Scarpetta said.

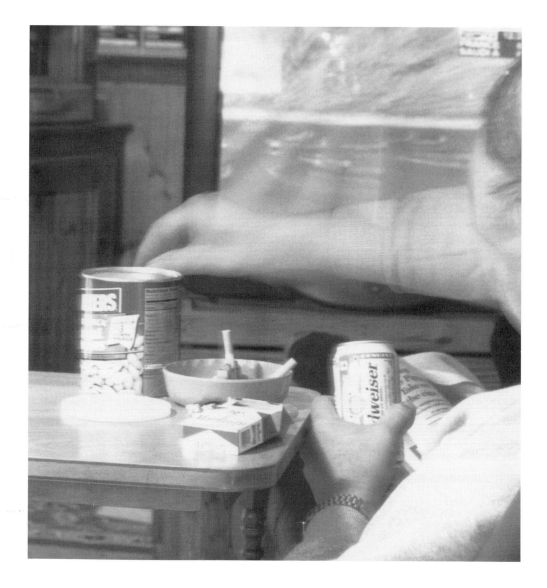

5

*I*n Richmond, at the precise moment Scarpetta was placing pasta in boiling water many miles south, Pete Marino was looking out at the weather. He was grateful his Dodge Ram Quad Cab pickup truck was safely under the aluminum carport. Otherwise it would, by now, be covered with at least three inches of snow—the soft, wet sort that he hated most. It inspired the neighborhood brats to fashion snowballs and hurl them in the direction of his small house in its quiet neighborhood south of the James River, just off Midlothian Turnpike.

These assaults inevitably occurred at night, resulting in soft thuds against windows, doors, and aluminum siding. By the time Marino was out on the porch, the suspects had fled, vanishing in the deep shadows of trees and to various residences along his street. He was an experienced officer of the law, and following footprints in snow was about as easy as arresting a rapist who leaves his wallet on the floor of the crime scene, or the thief who records his driver's license information on the back of the stolen check he's cashing. Oh yes, this had happened more times than well-behaved citizens would believe, but tracking children through the dark, frigid night, slipping and sliding, was a different matter altogether.

Marino lit a Marlboro and opened another can of Budweiser as he waited, ready in coat and boots, the television turned down low, an ear to the front of his house, as big flakes fell thickly. When he was growing up in New Jersey, he had committed far worse offenses than throwing snowballs at people. But in his case, violence was always justified and appropriate, for there were bullies and vandals in the blue-collar community of his youth. He had beaten the hell out of others only when he was picked on first or was protecting someone weaker. Marino was certain he had done nothing in this instance to justify the rude and thoughtless acts perpetrated by his small neighbors.

He had not factored in the many times he had chased them away from his above-ground swimming pool, or scattered them when they had dared to play football in his yard without asking. The occasions he had yelled and smacked a newspaper at the SPCA puppy that belonged one block away had not gone over very well, either, nor had the occasion when he had stopped his unmarked car and ordered Jimmy Simpson, who was ten, to pick up the candy wrapper he had just tossed on the street.

"You're lucky you aren't getting fined," he had told the blue-eyed boy.

"I'm not lost," Jimmy indignantly had said.

Marino believed, with no evidence, that Jimmy Simpson was the leader of the pack, and soon enough Marino would catch the vandal in the act and snatch him up by the scruff of his neck. He would march the boy into his single-parent residence and enlighten him and his mother about detention homes and jail.

The first artillery fire hit at exactly 8 P.M., snowballs pelting the front of the house. Marino didn't wait for a second round. Instantly he was out the front door, the enemy in sight. Jimmy Simpson was alone and no more than twenty feet from where Marino stood on the porch. Caught in the act, the boy was too frightened to run. He froze, eyes wide with terror. Marino stomped down the steps, his heavy boots crunching through snow.

"Just what the hell do you think you're doing?" he bellowed.

Jimmy began to cry. He cowered, arms in front of his face, as if he had been hit before by people bigger than he was.

"I knew it was you!" Marino severely went on, and he had reached the boy by now. "I've known it all along, you little scum bucket! What if you broke a window, huh?"

Jimmy was shaking as he sobbed.

"I didn't throw any at a window," his small voice barely said.

Marino had no evidence to the contrary.

"Yeah? Well, how would you like it if I threw snowballs at your house?" he gruffly said, his voice not quite as loud.

"I wouldn't care."

"Yes, you would."

"Would not."

"Well, your mother would care."

"Not if you didn't hurt anything."

"You're full of crap," Marino said, peering through snow at the milky smudges of windows lit up in Jimmy's two-bedroom brick home.

"You're not nice to me," Jimmy said, lowering his arms as fear began to leave him. "That's why! You started it!"

Marino had to think about this for a minute, his balding head getting cold.

"You mean that time I told you to get away from my pool?" Marino tried to remember.

The boy vigorously nodded.

"More than once!" Jimmy exclaimed. "And you give me mean looks when you pass me on the street in your police car."

"No, I don't."

"Do too."

"Only when you litter."

"That was one time! And there was chocolate all over the wrapper, and if I got it on my clothes, my mom would have gotten mad. So I dropped it by the road. So what!"

"What's your mom doing now?" Marino asked, as he began to feel something deep inside that made it hard for him to hate this lousy little kid.

"Stuck at her sister's house."

"Where's that?"

"I don't know," Jimmy quietly said, staring down at his feet. "I know it's near the park."

"Byrd Park?"

"The one with the lake and little boats. They sell cotton candy."

"She's not coming home?"

Jimmy shook his head.

"She said her car's stuck," he said.

"So you're all by your scrawny-ass self out here throwing snowballs."

"Yes, sir."

"You eaten yet?"

"Not since lunch."

"You like chili?"

"I don't know," Jimmy said.

"What about your mother's sister? Your aunt, I guess," he asked Jimmy.

"She's really my dad's sister."

"Should we call him?" Marino asked.

"No, sir. I don't know... He..."

Jimmy stared harder at his feet as snow frosted his hair. He was shivering in a denim jacket that was at least five sizes too big.

"Well, maybe you know your aunt's number?" Marino said.

"Uh-uh."

"Well, you sure as hell should."

"It's somewhere, I guess."

"Come on. Let's get out of the cold," Marino said.

They trudged through the yard and up Marino's front steps. He called Jimmy's house, and sure enough, no one was home. He left a message for Mrs. Simpson on the answering machine, saying that if it was all right with her, Jimmy would stay the night so he wouldn't have to be alone.

"I got Dr. Pepper, if you want some," Marino said, as he got ground beef out of the freezer.

Jimmy's eyes lit up.

"Sure!" he said.

MARINO'S LAST MINUTE CHILI

Marino's quick chili requires a number of considerations that differ from what most likely goes on in other kitchens. First, the chef should drink

Budweiser out of the can or Rolling Rock out of the bottle. Second, finding the appropriate pot requires digging and much clanging in jumbled cupboards, and locating the matching lid may not happen, in which case Marino fashions one from Reynolds Wrap. Third, the ground beef should be regular versus lean, and thawed in the microwave oven on high to hurry things along. The TV should be left on at all times, and one should be irritable when the phone rings.

"Mr. Marino?" said Jimmy, who was perched on a barstool. "Is it all right if I have some ice in my Dr. Pepper?"

"Nope, it ain't all right," Marino said.

He opened the freezer again and pulled out a frosted beer mug. He poured the Dr. Pepper in it while Jimmy's lips parted in awe.

"Be a man," Marino said.

"Cool!" was Jimmy's response.

Within half an hour, ground beef and bacon were browning in the pot. Marino was hacking up onions and green chili peppers, and opening cans of kidney beans, field peas, and Richfood tomato sauce.

"You ever eaten anything hot before?" Marino asked, as he chopped.

"Soup."

"Not that kind of hot."

"I don't know."

"Believe me, you'll know," Marino promised. "Let me tell you something, kid. Before the night's out, you're gonna learn something."

"You think there'll be school tomorrow, Mr. Marino?"

"Look, I'm either Captain Marino or Pete. Got it? And no way there'll be school tomorrow. I just hope your mom can get home so I'm not stuck with you another day."

Jimmy smiled. He knew Marino didn't mean it.

"I guess I could go get her in my truck," Marino went on.

"I'd rather stay here." Jimmy sipped his soda.

A more obvious ingredient in Marino's last minute chili is packaged seasoning. He prefers the very spicy Texas style, and dumps in two packages along with the tomato sauce he has on hand. In this case, it was three fifteen-ounce cans. To this he added an amount of water that he did not measure, but it wasn't a lot because he likes his chili thick enough to serve as spaghetti sauce when he needs a little variety. Next, he drained the beans and dumped them in, along with four beef bouillon cubes that initially stuck stubbornly to their wrappers.

"That smells really good," Jimmy marveled, as football players mauled each other on ESPN.

"Thirty minutes, and we're good to go," announced Marino, washing his hands and wiping them on his pants. "I got bread I can put some butter and garlic on, toast it in the oven."

"No, thank you."

"What about salad? Maybe I got some lettuce in here somewhere."

He searched inside the refrigerator, yanking open drawers.

"No, thank you," Jimmy replied. "I don't like salad."

"It's all in the dressing. You ever had Thousand Island? Mix mayonnaise, ketchup, and chop up bread and butter pickles. Mix it all up, put it on your salad, your burger, whatever. Now, you really want a manly meal, you make a really thick sandwich with corn beef and put Thousand Island and sauerkraut on it. Some Swiss if you got it. Hell, I've used mozzarella before. So you put that all together and grill it in butter."

"I don't like mayonnaise," Jimmy politely informed him.

"Won't even know it's there," Marino promised. "Maybe we'll do that for lunch tomorrow."

"I thought you didn't want me here."

"I don't," Marino said.

The snow had almost spent itself by the time the eleven o'clock news came on, and Marino was in his recliner, barely interested in what an anchor-woman was saying about a shooting in one of Richmond's numerous housing projects. It wasn't his problem. His jurisdiction was the police academy. He was in charge of training rookie cops and got involved in heinous, violent cases only when he was called out on an ATF or FBI response team.

"...the thus-far unidentified man was found face down on the street in a pool of blood..."

"Drugs," Marino muttered.

"...and is believed to be drug related..."

"See?" Marino said to Jimmy. "You know what that kind of homicide's called?"

The boy was stretched out on the brown vinyl couch, a blanket pulled up to his chin. Marino had given him a Richmond police academy T-shirt to sleep in, and the sleeves came down to Jimmy's hands, the hem over his feet.

"No, sir," Jimmy sleepily said.

"It's called *urban renewal.*"

"What does that mean?" Jimmy yawned.

"You'll figure it out when you get older. Sometimes we call them misdemeanor murders, too."

Jimmy was clueless.

"Oh," he said.

Marino took one last swallow of beer. That was his quota for the night. His guest had devoured two helpings of chili topped by melted mozzarella that had been stringy on Jimmy's spoon and had gotten on his face and sleeves, and everywhere, really. Marino had put out a plate of saltine crackers and had shown Jimmy how to crumble them into his bowl. For dessert, Marino had spread Chunky Monkey ice cream between two large sugar cookies, making a sandwich that Jimmy had dripped on his jeans.

"What are we having for breakfast?" Jimmy asked.

"Snow with maple syrup on it," Marino replied, switching to NBC.

"No way."

"It's okay as long as you stay away from yellow snow."

Jimmy Simpson guffawed.

Dessert was on Lucy's mind, and the longer she and her friends sat before the fire telling war stories about law enforcement and the cruelty of former lovers, the more it seemed a good idea for them to have one last forage before bed.

"Milk and cookies before bed," Lucy announced, getting up from the floor, where she had been lazily leaning against her aunt's handsome blue-and-maroon striped couch.

"Forget the milk part."

"Really."

"We'll figure out something," Lucy assured them. "You guys don't do anything fun without me. I'll be in the kitchen. And talk loud so I can hear everything you're saying."

LUCY'S FELONIOUS COOKIES

She set a deep Pyrex dish on the counter and hunted down brown and white sugar, all-purpose flour, vanilla extract, eggs, salt, and baking soda. When she was ten, her aunt had taught her to make these special, lawless cookies. By now, it was instinctive. Lucy never measured or timed anything. She had learned long ago to speed up the process and dirty as few dishes as possible. An important start was to melt a cup of Breakstone butter in the Pyrex dish, making sure the butter was warm but not hot.

Next, she stirred in dark brown and white sugar, forming a thick paste. Eggs followed, and her experience guided her to use two before mixing in enough flour to reach a moist, crumbly consistency that was neither too wet nor dry. Baking soda must not be overlooked, and she sprinkled in maybe a teaspoon of it before adding salt and vanilla to taste. By now, the dough was cool, and, with clean hands, Lucy kneaded in chopped pecans and semi-sweet chocolate and butterscotch chips. Although her aunt did not agree with her, Lucy believed in erring on the side of too much.

She turned on the oven to 350 degrees and lightly coated cookie sheets with a cholesterol-free vegetable oil that made Lucy smile. Her aunt was fastidious about good health.

"That's because you've seen so many dead people," Lucy frequently chided her, when Scarpetta would not buy her soft drinks or bubble gum or take her to fast-food restaurants except in an emergency.

During Lucy's many visits while she was growing up, there had always been fresh fruit juice in the refrigerator, and apples, bananas, tangerines, and white grapes. Popcorn at the movies was not a problem, but Scarpetta would not buy Lucy sweets, especially hard candies such as lemon drops or Fire Balls that potentially could choke. Suckers were out of the question, especially the sort from the bank or the doctor's office that were impaled on a hard stick.

"Imagine if you had that in your mouth and fell or ran into something," Scarpetta used to say.

"Why can't I just bite it off the stick?"

"Bad for your teeth. Actually, there's nothing about a lollypop that's of any benefit to you, Lucy. They don't even taste very good, if you think about it."

Perhaps it wasn't the lollypop as much as it was the fact that Lucy had been rewarded with it for enduring a tongue depressor halfway down her throat or waiting forever in line while her aunt deposited her state paycheck. The list of verboten foods and safety concerns got longer with time as her aunt discovered yet one more way someone could die. But Lucy's life with Scarpetta was not so severe as it might seem. Scarpetta had always given Lucy her time. Aunt Kay had enlightened and educated her with books, computers, and, now and then, church.

She had taught Lucy about good and evil, and had not tolerated selfishness, for it was, in Scarpetta's words, the root of all that was heartless and bad in the world.

Lucy formed small balls out of the cookie dough, which she first tasted raw, remembering when she was a kid and fat and had sneaked enough of it to make her sick. She flattened the balls just a little and placed them several inches apart on the cookie sheets.

"Someone get the Bailey's out of the bar. And glasses. Whiskey tumbler size," she directed from the doorway leading into the great room.

"You're sure your aunt doesn't mind us squatters wrecking her house?"

"We're not wrecking it," Lucy said.

"Not yet."

"When's she coming back?"

"Tomorrow, if planes can get in."

"What if we're still here?" An ATF agent, who knew all about bombs, laughed. "I mean, we might all be right here in this same spot, especially if we eat anything else."

"She won't care," Lucy said.

A second ATF agent eyed the holstered pistols and extra magazines scattered over tables.

"Wouldn't be a smart time for a burglar to show up," she matter-of-factly commented.

"OHHHH, all us women alone," Lucy said in a silly tone, as if she were ready for the fainting couch.

Normally, the cookies needed a good ten minutes in the oven, but Lucy always rescued them somewhat earlier than that, while they were still soft in the middle, because she liked them chewy and moist. With a spatula, she slid them onto a platter, eating one while it was hot.

"God," she groaned. "You're gonna die!" she called out to her friends. "They're so good they're bad!"

They dipped them into tumblers of Bailey's Irish Cream, sitting close to each other in front of the fire, the shadows of flames dancing on their faces.

The next morning, Marino did not serve Jimmy Simpson snow, as threatened, although he did jerk the boy around a bit by carrying a bowl of it into the house. He dribbled Mrs. Butterworth's maple syrup over it and stuck a soupspoon in the middle. Jimmy was warm with sleep and tangled in blankets on the couch when he opened his eyes and found Marino hovering over him, holding out the disgusting concoction.

"Snow cream," Marino told him.

Jimmy sat up, his dark tufts sprouting in different directions. He blinked several times, shifting into consciousness.

"Yuck," he said.

"How 'bout an omelet?" Marino asked. "Or you never had one of those, either?"

"I don't know."

Marino clicked on the TV. He opened the venetian blinds to let the overcast morning into his cramped, slovenly living room.

"I think it's going to snow again," Jimmy said, hopefully.

"Clouds aren't low enough," said Marino, the weather expert. "When they get low like fog and you can't see the sky anywhere, that's when you know. I can feel it like rain coming. Could happen before the day's out, though."

"Will I stay here again if it does?"

"One of these days your mother might want you back," Marino said.

MARINO'S SOUTHERN-STYLE NEW JERSEY OMELET

Marino was in a gray FBI sweat suit that did not completely cover his girth, and the feet of his white tube socks were stained orange from the insoles of his Gortex boots. He made his way into the kitchen, and soon enough had coffee brewing and was cracking eggs with one hand into a Tupperware juice container. The cast iron skillet was on the stove, and he wiped it with paper towels. He never washed the skillet with soap, and it was seasoned so well he didn't need to grease it.

The bacon had been used up the night before in the chili, so Marino had to be a little more creative about breakfast meat. He decided on Hebrew Brothers kosher knockwurst, splitting two and browning them in the skillet. These he put on a plate, which he covered with aluminum foil and placed in the oven, on warm. He poured several dollops of half-and-half into the juice container of eggs, added salt and pepper, and vigorously shook the mixture until it was frothy. He poured it into the skillet, and instantly the eggs began to cook around the edges and bubble in the middle.

The secret was to cook slowly and wait until there was no raw egg left. Then he turned the burner down to 150 degrees. He sliced cream cheese into thick squares and placed them in the middle of the omelet, which he expertly folded. A minute later, he turned the burner off entirely, and several minutes later the cream cheese was hot, the omelet ready to serve. He divided it, but certainly not equally, and, with a nod to the South, spooned strawberry preserves on top. He added the knockwurst to each plate and carried breakfast into the living room.

"How 'bout setting up those TV trays," he said, nodding at a rack of metal folding trays parked in a corner near the window.

Jimmy opened two of them, situating one in front of the recliner, the other where he was stationed on the couch.

"You can put mustard on your knockwurst, if you want," Marino said, cutting into his omelet.

"No, thank you."

"Let me know if you need more jelly."

"I like grape best," Jimmy confessed.

"Tough shit," Marino said.

9

*S*carpetta arrived on US Airways flight 301 after a typical changing of planes and dashing to distant gates in the Charlotte airport, where one was certain to stop on his way to anywhere else, including the afterlife. She had left her Mercedes in long term parking at Richmond's International Airport, and she was not able to open the driver's door at first because it was frozen shut, icicles on the handle.

Nor had she worn boots, because it had not occurred to her to pack them for her trip to Miami. Snow caved in around her loafers as she slipped and tugged. Eventually the door opened with a jerk, and now she was faced with cleaning off her car. She started the engine and turned the heat on high. She swiped the snow scraper over windshield, side and rear windows, and mirrors, meticulously clearing every inch of snow and ice off glass, for she was the last person on earth to drive with an obstructed view. How many cases had she seen where the victim died because of a blind spot? She got in and buckled up, driving defensively because not everyone else on the road felt the same way she did, or cared, frankly. They peered through arches left by sluggish wipers, great clumps of snow blowing off their roofs onto the windshields of cars behind them.

Scarpetta took I-64 West to the Fifth Street exit, eventually winding around on the Downtown Expressway, passing her old building at Fourteenth and Franklin Streets. She did not miss working in the ugly four-story precast concrete building with its small windows and biological hazards, but reminders of the past brought so much to mind. She thought of stages she had passed through, of Lucy as a child, and relationships that had left their marks. Scarpetta thought of the dead, too, of those who had come under her care and once were front-page news. She could not remember every name, but she could still see her patients in her mind and recall the smallest details of what she had learned about them. The smokestacks on the roof of her old building were forlorn and cold. The crematorium had been quiet for years.

The streets of Windsor Farms were rutted and deep with slush that would turn to ice with the fading day. She moved slowly along Dover Road into the newer neighborhood, where she lived. The guard in his booth was named Roy, and he waved her through, always happy to see her because she appreciated why he was there and told him so regularly. She understood the dangers out-side wrought iron fences and brick walls. More often than she liked to think, Roy had deterred the unsavory and the curious from finding her. It pleased her to see Lucy's old green Suburban and the cars of friends in the drive. Miami had been miserable, and sometimes snow made Scarpetta lonely. The thought of company lifted her mood.

She unlocked the front door and walked inside the foyer, setting luggage on the hardwood floor.

"We're in here," Lucy called out.

"Welcome home!"

"Thanks for letting us stay!"

Scarpetta followed cheery voices into the great room, where the women were still worthless around the fire, their pistols and other weapons out in plain view. Blankets, pillows, beer bottles, and whiskey tumblers were a mess on the rug.

"All of us slept in here last night," Lucy explained to her aunt.

"Sounds like fun," Scarpetta said.

"Too much fun."

"The cookies are what did it."

"Try what they were dipped in. That's what did it."

"Dr. Scarpetta, we'll clean up our mess and be on our way. Thanks again."

"Don't rush off because of me," she said. "The roads will be freezing soon, and it looks like it might snow again. I don't think any of you need to be in your cars."

She meant this for reasons other than the weather.

"We've been good so far today," Lucy assured her. "Just coffee and diet sodas. But you're right." She looked at her friends. "I don't think you guys need to be heading back north."

Scarpetta glanced at her watch. It was not quite 3 P.M. There was just enough time to make her famous stew.

SCARPETTA'S FAMOUS STEW

The *sine qua non* is a restaurant-size pot capable of holding twenty quarts. Usually—and this day was no exception—Scarpetta had two going at once, as the abundance of ingredients she used simply could not be contained in a single vessel. Meat was her first priority, and she pulled ground turkey, cubed tenderloin trimmed of all fat, veal, and chicken breasts from the freezer. These she placed in the microwave oven to thaw. Unlike Marino, she did not rush the process. There was plenty else to do.

Over Lucy's protests, Annie Lennox and Meat Loaf were replaced by Pachelbel, Beethoven, and Mozart. Scarpetta opened two bottles of red table wine and began raiding her refrigerator, cupboards, and pantry for whatever her imagination seized upon. Without a doubt, the most important clue when making Scarpetta's stew is that the essence of it comes from her; the rest belongs to you. Use what you have and make the best of it, but as is true of any homicide case, it's only as good as the evidence brought in. So if you're stingy with your time and what you invest in your stew, what you cook is what you'll get.

Without question, this spectacularly hearty and loving dish requires work. Scarpetta tied an apron around her waist and began chopping Vidalia onions, red and yellow and green bell peppers, fresh oregano, basil, and parsley. She sliced baby carrots, squash, asparagus, fresh mushrooms, and pulled the strings from snow peas. Peeled Hanover tomatoes she had canned herself were not something she parted with every day, for once they were gone there were no more until summer. She pried off lids and mixed them and everything else in a huge glass bowl. She painstakingly peeled husks from the cloves of two large garlic bulbs and got to work with the garlic press. This, and salt and fresh ground pepper she stirred in with the vegetables.

She poured no more than a tablespoon of olive oil into each pot and turned the heat to medium. By now the meat was thawed enough to work with, and she crumbled equal shares of ground turkey into each pot and cut the tenderloin and chicken into small pieces. While this browned, she began opening jars of V-8 juice and cans of tomato sauce. It is important to note that the three most important elements in her stew are the tomato base, garlic, and red wine. These should be used liberally to taste, but without an extravagant amount of each, the stew will not bear Scarpetta's signature.

By 4 P.M., she was pouring herself a glass of the table wine and dividing the rest of the bottle between the two pots. At five o'clock, the stew was bubbling and permeating the house, and she poured a glass of wine from the second bottle. The rest went into the pots, which she covered with lids, turning down the heat. Even the slightest hint of scorching will ruin her stew. Again, patience is essential. It is true that the best things in life require a bit of a wait.

"It's going to have to cook for a while," Scarpetta told her guests, as she walked into the great room, drying her hands on her apron.

"I can tell you right now, it's worth it," Lucy promised her friends.

"A little later, I'll make bread," Scarpetta went on. "We'll eat around eight. Tomorrow, if you're here for lunch, the stew will be even better."

Ideally, it needed to simmer for at least five hours.

"Can't we help with something?" one of the ATF agents asked.

"No." Scarpetta smiled. "It's no good unless I do it myself. If any other hands get involved, something goes wrong. It never fails. And by all means don't ever use expensive wine," she added, as she returned to the kitchen. "It doesn't like that, either."

"*It?*" the FBI agent puzzled.

"Every stew has its own personality," Lucy explained. "Like people. It's really strange, but each batch kind of reflects where Aunt Kay is coming from."

"You mean she *projects* herself onto it?"

"It *channels* through her?"

"Some kind of Taoist thing?"

"Kind of like that," Lucy said.

"Makes sense, really. The same way someone's clothes or the way they decorate their house fits who they are."

"Yeah," Lucy said. "And the more peppery it is, the more you'd better run for cover."

"What about garlic?"

"Wards off bad spirits. The more she uses, the more stuff's going on that she probably hasn't told you about," Lucy replied.

"What if she chops up more raw meat than usual?"

"Or puts on surgical mask and gloves to cut up vegetables?"

"Or sections the gizzards?"

The women were getting silly.

"We should invite Marino over," Lucy suggested.

"I thought you said the roads were bad."

"He's got a truck with chains," Lucy said.

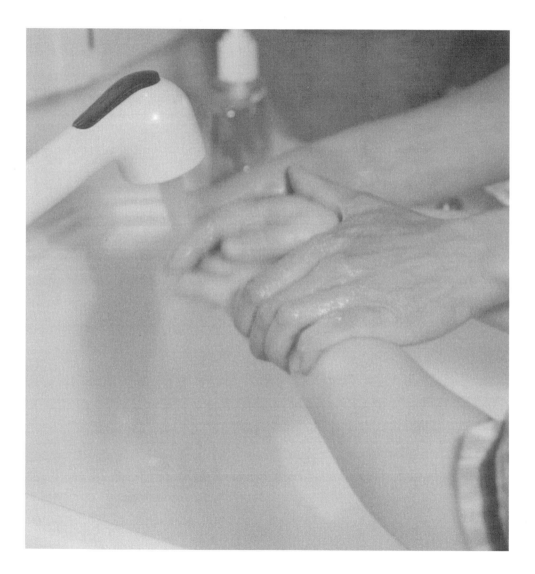

Marino had picked up Mrs. Simpson and was dropping Jimmy and her off at their home when Lucy rang his portable phone.

"What 'chu doin', dude?" Lucy loudly asked.

"Who's this?" Marino demanded, as if he didn't know.

"Your snitch, man."

"Which one?"

"Can't tell you over a cellular phone, dirt bag. Ten-twenty-five me in the West End at the usual spot."

"Hold on a minute," Marino said, covering the phone with a big meaty hand.

Jimmy and his mother were sitting in the truck, the boy in front, she in back.

"You guys have a good night, okay?" Marino said. "And listen here, you little runt." He poked his finger at Jimmy. "One more snowball at my house, and it's all over. Juvenile court. Death row. Get it?"

Jimmy wasn't the least bit scared, but suddenly he looked sad. His mother was very quiet and seemed too young to have a child of any age. She was bundled in an old corduroy coat with a fake fur collar, her face tired and pale.

Marino changed his mind.

"Hold on," Marino said to them. "Hey, listen up," he then said into the receiver. "Get the doc on the phone."

Scarpetta got on the line.

"Where are you and why aren't you here?" she asked. "I'm cooking stew."

"Shit. I'm gonna have the big one," Marino said, and he might have meant it. "I knew you'd be cooking something. You always do after you been around your old lady and whacko sister."

"Please watch your language," Scarpetta told him.

"You got enough for two more people?"

"Have you done background checks on them?" she asked.

"I'm not too sure of the kid," Marino said, giving Jimmy a look that was supposed to be hard and terrifying. "But I'll keep my eye on him."

This was fine. In fact, Scarpetta knew Marino well enough to sense that his guests were special and in need of warmth and nourishment. He had brought strangers over before, but never anyone who might harm her.

Chains cut into ice, clanking rhythmically as he pulled out of the Simpsons' driveway and followed the street to Midlothian Turnpike and soon was chopping through I-95 North and taking the West Cary Street exit. Very few people were out, and really, no one should have been. Marino kept his speed down to no more than forty miles per hour.

"Why are you doing all this for us?" Mrs. Simpson quietly asked.

"You got your seat belt fastened?" It was more an order than an inquiry, as he eyed her in the rearview mirror.

"Just like it was a minute ago," she said.

"He made me an omelet this morning," Jimmy bragged to his mother. "With cheese in it and jelly. And he likes Cocoa Puffs, too. I saw a box on top of his refrigerator. He's really cool!"

"Cocoa Puffs aren't good for you." Mrs. Simpson sounded tired when she spoke.

"Sure they are, if you slice a banana on top of 'em," Marino answered, as he carefully turned onto a narrow, tree-lined street.

He stopped at the guard booth and rolled down his window to greet Roy, who was still on duty this snowy winter's night.

"Keeping trouble out?" Marino asked, lighting a cigarette.

"Just these Cadillacs sliding everywhere." Roy shook his head. "One of them's gonna hit the gate, I just know it."

"I guess if you live in a high-dollar neighborhood like this, the weather don't affect you, right?"

Roy laughed, glad that none of the homeowners, who paid his salary through their monthly dues, could hear him having fun at their expense.

"You eaten yet?" Marino asked him.

"Not 'til I get off at midnight."

"You hungry?"

"I can't go anywhere," Roy reminded him.

"Don't need to," Marino told him.

The windows were lit up in Scarpetta's well-appointed home, and now that Marino's pickup was added to the cars in the drive, it was beginning to look like a party or a tow lot. Mrs. Simpson almost lost her balance when she stepped out on the running board. She had never been in a neighborhood like this, much less invited inside a house so fine. She was suddenly intimidated, but the lady who opened the front door dispelled any insecurities or doubts. A Christmas green apron covered her slacks and turtleneck, and she was handsome, blond, blue-eyed, and somewhere in the middle years of her life. Her smile was warm and kind.

"Please come in," Scarpetta said, as if she had been waiting for them long before they had ever met. "I'm Kay."

"I'm Jimmy and this is my mom."

"So *you're* the one throwing snowballs," Scarpetta wryly said to him.

"Yes, ma'am," he politely said. "But I didn't try to hit him."

"Maybe next time you should."

"Yes, ma'am."

"Then what happens to you, huh?" Marino poked him.

"Same thing that happened last time, Captain. Nothing." Jimmy was full of himself.

He and his mother were trying not to stare, not sure where to let their eyes rest. There were antique microscopes and apothecary scales, old books and beautiful paintings, so much to look at.

"I've never seen a house this big before," Jimmy told Scarpetta.

"Well, I'll be glad to give you a tour," she said.

"How 'bout you let me take a bowl of stew to Roy?" Marino asked.

"There's plenty for everyone," Scarpetta said.

"You can give me a hand," Marino told Mrs. Simpson, as if he had known her for quite some time.

"What?" She was startled.

"There are Tupperware containers above the stove," Scarpetta said to them. "You two take care of Roy, and I'll get Jimmy to help me out in the kitchen."

"Come on." Marino nodded at Mrs. Simpson. "The rule around this joint is you gotta earn your keep."

"I always earn my keep," she said, with a trace of defiance.

"Oh yeah?" He tugged her sleeve, moving her into the kitchen. "You like to bowl?"

"Before Hank left...I...I used to belong to a league. The Lucky Strikes. I'm pretty good."

"You ever heard of the Silvertips?"

"No."

"As in ammo. Hollowpoints-Plus P."

She had no idea what he was talking about. She removed the lid from the big pot on the stove. The stew was simmering and looked delicious.

"You want to stop somebody, that's what you use," he cheerfully went on, for bowling and ammunition were two of his favorite subjects. "Real destructive, in other words. Like the way we bowl."

"I see," she said.

She picked up a ladle and felt more at home as she began to fill the Tupperware container while Marino shook a cigarette out of his pack.

"I can never do those damn lids," he said, as he watched her. "You ask me, they don't fit right."

"You have to burp it," said Mrs. Simpson with a sudden rush of confidence. "Just like that." She showed him. "Men are too impatient. That's the problem. Not to mention, it's worth your while to be worthless in the kitchen."

Marino noticed for the first time that Jimmy's mother had smooth skin and bright hazel eyes. Her hair was a deep chestnut and shaggy around her shoulders, the way he liked it.

"You got a first name?" he asked.

"Abby."

"I'm Pete. You want to walk with me to the guard booth?"

"That would be nice," she said.

"Your coat warm enough?"

"As warm as it's ever been."

"You can wear my gloves."

He pulled leather gloves lined with rabbit fur out of his pocket. Abby Simpson could have fit both her hands in one of them. Suddenly, she started laughing.

"You must've been a Boy Scout," she said, feeling giddy.

"Nope," he said, "a juvenile delinquent."

"*Silvertips!*" She laughed harder, her eyes tearing up.

They walked out the door into the snow. Steam from the container of hot stew and smoke from Marino's cigarette dispersed into the dark, sharp air.

"Your kid's pretty cool," Marino confessed to her.

"You think I should have left him there?" she asked, as they made their way past grand, silent houses with windows lit up. "I don't want him to be a pest."

"Too late for that," Marino told her.

Jimmy had never been inside a kitchen like Scarpetta's, although he had seen pictures of similar ones in the magazines his mother bought at the grocery store. When

Scarpetta opened a drawer and pulled out a roll of oven-strength Reynolds Wrap, he was suddenly afraid. He didn't know what to say to her. She was very smart and important. He could tell.

"Here's what we have to do," she began, as she tied an apron around his waist. "Now, don't be a tough guy and get nervous, all right? Some of the best cooks are men, and they wear aprons, and there's not a thing wrong with that."

Jimmy stared down at the stiff black apron wrapped around him. It hung below his knees and had a colorful crest on it.

"My special apron," she added. "I don't let just anybody wear it."

"How is it special?" He was glad Marino couldn't see him right now.

"It has my crest on it." She opened the oven door, and a wave of heat and the aroma of baking bread made Jimmy feel warm and happy.

"What's a crest?" he asked.

"Hmmm." She tried to think of a good analogy as she used potholders to lift the pan out of the oven and set it on the stove. "Sort of like the symbols you see for Nike, Speedo, the Atlanta Braves, the Redskins. Something that stands for a person, a team, a brand—whatever."

"What do you want me to do with the tinfoil?" asked Jimmy.

"We're going to wrap the bread in foil to keep it warm until Marino and your mom get back."

"They sure are taking a long time," he said.

Scarpetta tapped the sides of the bread pan with the handle of a knife. "That's to loosen it. Now I turn it over like this, and there we are."

The bread was golden brown and perfectly shaped. Jimmy tore off a long sheet of foil, his nails ragged and dirty and chewed to the quick. When he saw her looking, he quickly shoved his hands into the pockets of his jeans and felt his cheeks heat up.

"I'm assuming you've been to the doctor and the dentist," she said, as she set the bread on the foil.

"Yes, ma'am. They give shots."

"You notice how doctors and dentists scrub up?"

"I don't know."

"They wash their hands a lot," she explained. "Very carefully. I do, too. In fact, I must wash my hands at least a dozen times a day when I'm working."

"Oh," he said.

"To kill germs and so forth."

"Mom says germs are teeny little worms you can't see. They crawl inside you if you don't take a bath or brush your teeth."

"In a way she's right." Scarpetta moved a step stool close to the sink. "Stand on this," she directed.

He was uncertain as he stepped up, but it felt fine to be as tall as she was.

"Here we go," she said. "I used to have to do the same thing for Lucy. No matter what she did, somehow she got dirty."

Scarpetta began washing Jimmy's hands. It felt very good, but he would never tell her such a thing. When she finished, she dried them with a clean dishtowel. He stepped down and looked up at her, wondering what to expect next.

"Are you hungry?" she asked.

"Yes, ma'am, a little." His stomach had retreated into its empty place, and the sights and smells in Scarpetta's kitchen were unbearably wonderful. "But I can wait," he added.

Scarpetta poured him a glass of milk, sat him at the kitchen table, and draped a cloth napkin over his lap. He watched her stir the stew and grate hard yellow cheese. Then she unwrapped the bread and cut off an end piece—his favorite part—and slathered it with butter. She fetched shakers from a cupboard and coated the hot, buttered bread with cinnamon sugar and a dash of cocoa powder.

"I call this *cappuccino bread*." She winked at him and smiled.

She placed his treat under the broiler for a minute and served it to him crusty and bubbling hot.

"Of course, this is against all my rules. It will probably ruin your dinner."

"Oh no, ma'am."

"It will be our secret." She sat at the table with him.

"I won't tell," he said.

Jimmy wanted to be polite and eat slowly, chewing small bites, as his mother had taught him. But in seconds the bread was gone and warming his stomach. He wiped his hands on his jeans.

"I'm not giving you any more," she told him.

"That's all right." He felt very shy and didn't want her to think it would ever occur to him to want more, even though he did.

"Because you need to eat your stew. And a salad, too."

"Yes, ma'am, I will," he assured her. "I can eat a lot. A whole lot."

"You ever seen a microscope?" Scarpetta asked him, as they got up from the table.

"What's a microscope?" he asked.

"Something that makes small things very big," she said, taking his hand.

They walked out of the kitchen together.

Since the fun of this is that no concoction will ever be the same, you are encouraged to take notes.

Kay Carpenter, M.D.

_____

_____

_____

_____

_____

_____

_____

_____

_____

_____

_____

_____

_____

_____

Also by Patricia Cornwell